BenJamin
ALeXanDer
SHeeP
a STOrY

Bob Friedman

**cover design
and illustration
by Jim Lamb**

A Division of G/L Publications
Glendale, California, U.S.A.

Other Regal books by Bob Friedman include:
Pursued
What's a Nice Jewish Boy Like You
    Doing in the First Baptist Church?

© Copyright 1973 by G/L Publications
All rights reserved
Printed in U.S.A.

Published by
Regal Books Division, G/L Publications
Glendale, California 91209, U.S.A.

Library of Congress Card No. 73-83731
ISBN 0-8307-0264-4

Part One

Benjamin Alexander Sheep
dipped his head to within an inch of the pond
and opened his mouth as wide as he could.
There! Two teeth, large and straight, had replaced the old ones in the center. Maybe now
that stupid Gridley would stop teasing him
about being a baby lamb.

Benjie looked into the water again. On each
side of his new ones there remained three milk
teeth. In three more years, when he was about
four, Benjie would have a full mouth of fine
teeth.

And then a most horrible feeling came over
him.

Three more years? Three more years of putting
up with that stupid ram Gridley, and taking

orders from the older ones in the flock? Three more years of being pushed into following a large ewe while grazing?

Benjamin Alexander Sheep had nothing against togetherness, but the boldness that comes with your first pair of adult teeth swept through him and gave him courage. He was tired of following. He wanted to lead.

The falling sun played tricks on the sloping pasture, and Benjie soon discovered the light which was bouncing off those distant objects revealed a cluster of boulders instead of the sheep he had expected.

OK, Benjie, he said to himself, *stay calm. You'll find them.* But instead of looking further he was content to hungrily gobble a clump of short, fine grass. A welcome change from the weeds he had found the day before.

With his stomach full of fresh water and choice grass the yearling slumped to the ground and fell asleep just as the sun dropped behind the curved horizon of the vast land.

He was awakened the next morning by a harsh, raspy sound and then a heavy *whack* as a wooden crook landed on his rump.

"C'mon, you lazy little twerp. Get up! Up, I say!"

Benjamin didn't even have time to stretch or scratch his belly. Cragmire, the tall, loping shepherd, had hooked him around his neck and lifted him with one hand so only Benjie's back legs were scraping along.

"Baaaaa!" Benjamin protested.

"Baaaaa, yourself!" the shepherd said.

Benjamin slipped on the dew-soaked grass, felt another *whack* just above his tail bone, then quickly scrambled to his feet and away from the laughing Cragmire.

It was later that day, as Benjie was shoved to and fro within the flock, that he seriously began thinking of a way of escape from Gridley, Cragmire and the others.

He knew he couldn't strike out on his own. Sheep simply couldn't do that. They, of all animals, were completely dependent upon man. As Benjie became tangled in his thoughts he felt a slight push on his right flank. A different kind of push. A gentle one.

It was Lana Lee.

"Hi, Lana!"

"Oh, hi, Benjie. I didn't see you. Eating as we walk along and all that . . ."

Didn't see him, indeed! Lana Lee had been born just a week after Benjie, and right from the first he knew she liked him. You could always tell these things. Once she just happened to drop half of a turnip by him, and another time she was wondering if Benjie would be as fine a ram as his father was.

"What's happening, little one?" Benjie asked.

He formed his mouth into a small circle so only his two new teeth could be seen.

"Are you all right?" she asked.

"Sure. Why?"

"Your face looks funny."

"Oh. I'm, uh, just trying to free some brush that's stuck between my teeth."

Benjie was very glad that short, fine hair covered his skin below his eyes and around his nose and mouth for he unavoidably blushed. Then, as he was about to speak, Lana Lee crashed against him and they both went tumbling into the others.

"Watch out!"

"Knucklehead!"

"Clumsy!"

Benjie and Lana Lee looked up into the face of a very large and grinning ram. It was Gridley.

"That's not funny, Gridley!"

"Why, Benjie baby! Is the little lamb all

upset?" He broke into uncontrollable laughter and, as Benjie attempted to stand, pushed him over again with his large head.

"Cut it out, Gridley," Lana pleaded.

"My, my," Gridley continued, "baby Benjie has a baby ewe speaking for him. But not a bad looking ewe at that. What's your name, sweetheart?"

"None of your business, you dumb ram!" Benjie was on his feet and faced Gridley, his entire body becoming lost in the ram's long shadow.

"C'mon, Benjamin. Show me how brave you are!" Gridley's lips curled back over his bared teeth.

"Benjie, no!" Lana Lee cried.

Benjie swallowed hard and gave a quick glance at Lana. He wanted more than anything else to show her how brave he was, to be better than Gridley. But as he nervously examined the

ram's lowered horns and dark, piercing eyes, he knew it was no use.

"I don't have to fight you," his voice shook with anger, "I'll be better than you someday! I'll be bigger! And stronger! I'll lead and you'll follow!"

"Oh, sure, Benjie," Gridley said, "and life will be just one big pasture full of mangels and rutabagas. You'd have a better chance if you tried to match wits with Cragmire or turn your fleece to a pure white."

He didn't know if it was out of desperation, fear or a strange kind of bravado. Maybe if Lana Lee hadn't been watching it would have been different, or if he hadn't felt his new teeth on his tongue before he spoke.

But in any case Benjamin Alexander Sheep lifted his broad head as high as he could, filled his chest with air, and with a strange, cool voice accepted Gridley's last challenge.

"If I can change my fleece to a pure white, Gridley," Benjamin said, "then you'll follow me?"

Gridley took a step backwards and cocked his head. Benjamin almost sounded as if he was serious.

"Benjie baby," Gridley gulped, with his voice a higher pitch than he would have liked, "if you can turn your fleece into a pure white I'll fall down at your hoofs and worship you."

Benjamin and Lana Lee lay side by side, looking into the still pond. Once in a while one would turn and lick a small lump of salt Lana had taken from Cragmire when he had fallen asleep in the late afternoon warmth.

Cold clear water. Salt. A pretty ewe. A lazy day. All of the ingredients for a fine time were spread before Benjie, but no matter how hard he tried he couldn't get Gridley off his mind.

Why did he say what he did? Why did he make a fool out of himself and promise to turn his fleece to a pure, bright white? He had seen fleeces which were only slightly gray, or once a stray lamb passed through who had an almost pure black fleece. Never pure white.

Benjamin dipped his head into the water, took a drink, then splashed his eyes with a quick jerk of his head.

That lamb with the black fleece must be a lot better off than most of them, he thought. At least he was definite. He made a statement about something. He was black. You knew where he stood.

The shades of gray were always confusing. The light grays thought the darker grays were inferior, because the dark grays could never make it to black, thereby maintaining a special identity, and at the same time they were farther away from a true white.

The darker grays thought, in turn, that they were superior to the light grays since they *were* closer to a definitive black and, after all, true white was only a mere illusion never to be realized.

"Benjamin?"

"Yeah, Lana?"

"Nothing."

She'd do this often. Make him press her to reveal her thoughts. So many times he had wanted to let her have the last word and call her bluff, but his curiosity always won out. It bothered him terribly that Lana Lee knew this.

"Let's have it."

"Have what?"

"What you're thinking."

"It's nothing."

Uh, oh. Must be important. The game usually ended after the first round unless it really was an urgent issue.

"Lana!"

"All right!" She took a long, long drink. "It's just that, that I don't know exactly what's come over you. Telling Gridley you'd made your fleece white and all that."

"It's possible, isn't it?"

"Yes. I suppose so. But . . . I . . ."

"But, what?"

"I don't think you can do it," then, quickly, "or anyone else here for that matter!"

"Thanks a lot!" Benjamin stood, staring downward at Lana Lee, and half-turned away as he threatened to leave.

"Benjamin, wait!"

Lana Lee hopped to her feet. Her usual shy, timid self was temporarily put aside and an eagerness Benjie had never seen before flooded her large, brown eyes.

For a few moments they just faced each other, both afraid to speak. Benjamin's back was toward the pond and his rear feet rested in a couple of inches of water.

"Benjie, listen," Lana began, "I didn't say you *wouldn't* have a pure white fleece some day, or *couldn't* have one. I just said you couldn't do it by yourself. That's all."

"Then who's going to help me? Gridley?" Lana Lee was so silly at times that Benjamin couldn't believe it. Can't do it by himself!

"No, not Gridley."

"Then who?"

Lana Lee began to walk around the edge of the pond, stopping every now and then for a taste of grass or drink of water out of nervousness rather than thirst or hunger. Benjamin instinctively followed.

"Have you ever studied the pond, Benjie? Or a blade of grass?"

Benjamin knew she didn't take the direct approach, but this was quite ridiculous. One minute they're speaking of the color of fleeces, the next minute she's wandered off onto a nature kick.

"No, Lana Lee," Benjie said with an air of great tolerance mixed with undisguised sympathy, "I have never studied the pond—or a blade of grass."

"You should, really." Benjie braced himself.

"Why?"

"Just because."

"Lana, I'm really not in the mood for . . ."

"See how gentle the grass is? Yet it's strong enough to push up through the hardest ground. And although it doesn't look like much it tastes so good. Much better than those high weeds which are so hard to chew."

"Lana, I'm beginning to think that . . ."

"And the water! Just as the pond gets low a rain comes and fills it up again!"

"Lana? Were you listening when old Cragmire

gave us a lesson on what loco weed looked like? Maybe you . . ."

"Oh, Benjamin! Think! Think!"

She began to shed great lamb's tears. They fell below her eyes before being stopped by curly tufts of wool which grew on each side of her face. As she stood there Benjie's eyes drifted over her body. She really was a beautiful ewe. Her rump was level and she had spotless legs, a broad head and a very deep flank. She'd give birth to many fine lambs one day.

"Lana, whatever it is you want to say, please say it."

"I ca . . . can't," she sobbed.

"And why not?"

"You'd . . . you'd laugh at me."

"Try me."

"I can't! Why can't you see without my telling you? You'll laugh. I know you'll laugh!"

At this point Lana Lee turned and ran away as fast as she could. Benjamin, stunned, watched her disappear over a rise in the meadow.

That evening Benjie spotted his parents, a fine old ram and a very respected ewe, standing together near the outside of the flock. Although he had had a number of wives, some say in the hundreds, Benjamin's father was partial to his mother.

"Hello, Benjamin."

"Maw."

"Son."

"Hi, Dad."

"Say, have you heard about Prissy?" Mrs. Alexander Ram said. "That stupid old ewe got lost again yesterday and Cragmire brought her back. Gave her a real licking, too. She probably deserved it."

"No sheep deserves to have its wool pulled out," the old ram said. "She's probably bleeding from torn tissue or skin."

"It's the only way Cragmire could pull her out of that ditch. He said so."

Something inside Benjie stirred up a fresh sense of uneasiness and he decided to challenge his mother for the first time in his life.

"Just like that?" Benjamin said angrily. "You believe Cragmire just like that?"

"Why . . . of course, Benjie." His mother's jaw fell slightly and, as is his habit when something unusual has taken place, the ram turned his left horn toward the speaker.

"He's the shepherd, son," Mr. Alexander Ram said.

"So?"

The two older sheep blinked at each other. Benjamin had always been such a good boy.

Following the flock, eating his share and no more. Not straying too far from the others.

"Well . . .," the mother said, *"he's the shepherd!"*

"I thought the shepherd was supposed to love and take care of the flock!" Benjamin said.

"He does, doesn't he?" asked the ram.

"What about Prissy?"

"Maybe . . . maybe that's the only way he could get her out of the ditch."

"Dad, do you really believe that?"

"No," he whispered.

Benjie slowly walked up his favorite hill in order to bed down for the night. He liked it as high as possible. He ignored all attempts at conversation the other sheep started. He closed his eyelids, pretending to be asleep, even though his mind would not yet yield to this luxury.

Steady, Benjamin Alexander Sheep, he said. *Let's review what's happened.*

First, that ugly Gridley. And the promise Benjie had made to make his fleece all white. If he couldn't pull this off he had to find another flock, for it would be unbearable to continue the verbal harassment day after day.

Second—Lana Lee. That crazy ewe almost sounded as if she knew something he didn't, but before she could get it out her thoughts were drowned in a typically female rush of tears. The wool under her eyes would be soaked all night.

Third—his parents. The mere fact Cragmire was shepherd was reason enough to justify all of his actions. Yet, when confronted, the old ram was too wise to admit this. A very strange thing indeed.

Steady, Benjie, get your head together. OK.

Now. Course of action, right? Let's say, for argument's sake, that one had to be practical and concede that he, being a sheep, most definitely needed a shepherd.

But Cragmire was the only shepherd around. There were no others. So—here's the problem. A shepherd is needed—Cragmire is the only shepherd—but Cragmire simply will not do.

Most importantly, Cragmire could not supply Benjamin with a pure white fleece.

The grass began to itch him through the thick, rippled wool. Bugs? Wind? Neither, thought Benjie. Probably a restless mind. He twisted his body around and tucked his head into a more comfortable position.

Then, as if he was expecting it, a strange idea began to echo in his head. He couldn't tell if it actually was an unfamiliar voice or his own thoughts which suddenly burst forth and brought him to a new level of enlightenment.

The feeling which surrounded him was also strange. The kind of feeling he had once when he snatched a carrot away from another lamb who was in no position to fight back.

The carrot tasted so very, very good, yet because he had obtained it in such a devious way a new dimension of thrill accompanied each bite. Doing something he shouldn't be doing, yet not feeling sorry he's doing it because of the great pleasure it brought.

The voice, or whatever it was, had gone, but the impression it had left was most definite.

If Benjie, it said, could become his *own* shepherd he would have his white fleece and be rid of Cragmire at the same time! Benjie was the only leader that Benjie ever needed!

It was sheer nonsense to think he really needed someone to look out for him. Especially if his fleece was pure white. For this would demand so much respect from the others, and such a following, that he would be considered a *true* shepherd. One the other sheep could identify with.

Tomorrow, he thought, he would begin to work for his white fleece. Soon Gridley would only be one of the many worshiping him day and night.

And Benjamin drifted off into a deep, deep sleep.

Part Two

For Benjie,
his first idea was an obvious one. He had seen Cragmire take a large pile of cloth and skins to the edge of the river and furiously scrub them up and down until they came out looking much brighter than when they had gone in.

If Cragmire could do it, so could Benjie. And although he couldn't actually *rub* himself in the water, he could let the water soak his wool long enough to insure a pure white fleece.

Benjie tip-toed to the edge of the slowly moving river and dipped his front right hoof into the water. Then the front left. He hated rainwater which drenched his coat and ran down his back, causing him to shiver and bleat for Cragmire to throw a skin over him for protection. This would be far worse.

All four feet were in. So far so good. The water was very shallow where he stood, thereby allowing him to painfully lower himself until the water flowed over his back but below his head.

His head! Benjie had almost forgotten. It wouldn't do to have a white fleece and a gray head. Then the others would *really* laugh. He decided to dip his head into the water every few moments to make sure his entire body would be transformed.

It could have been five minutes or five hours, Benjie was too cold and miserable to take notice. In any case, the sun had moved to the top of the sky and Benjie felt as if he weighed at least two thousand pounds. Surely, after all this time, his fleece would now be white.

Benjamin climbed very laboriously out of the river. His saturated fleece hindered his every move. With great hope and anticipation he ducked his head very low to check out the color of his chest and front feet.

The matted, dripping wool was most definitely the very same gray Benjie had always seen.

He lifted his head high and felt the strong rays of the sun begin to call the water from his fleece. He stood there, with his eyes closed, and once again determined to complete his task.

He stood there, in the sun, and promised not to move until he was completely dry.

He stood there, in the sun, long after his wool was its usually springy self and waited.

And waited and waited for the sun to bleach his light gray covering to a whiter-than-white newness.

Benjie was very, very hungry. He had not

grazed all day and there would be only about a half hour left before the pasture once again leaped up and covered the daily light.

With eyes closed his head bobbed over the sweet grass. Why look now? In a few minutes it would be too dark to see very well and the suspense could be sustained until the next morning.

It was much better this way. Hope ceased to be hope once the thing hoped for was found.

Benjie kept grazing as he worked his way up his favorite hill. As he finally lay down in the darkness an unfamiliar voice addressed him.

"Are you Benjamin?" the voice said.

"Yes, who are you?"

"I'm part of the flock. But I only come near at night."

"Why?"

"Just because . . ."

"Just because what?" Benjie asked.

"You wouldn't understand."

"Try me."

There was a certain sweet-sadness about the other's voice. A kind of helplessness mixed with understanding most sheep wouldn't appreciate.

"Well, I'm a very black sheep!"

"You are!"

"Now don't run off like the others do," he pleaded, "please hear what I have to say."

"Sure," Benjie said, "but why do the others run off?"

"Because they think I feel superior, having a fleece of such a definite color."

"I always thought so, too. As a matter of fact I'm . . ."

"But that's not really the case," the other broke in, "for if any sheep stood still long enough to ask me how I felt, I'd have to admit I was very sad."

"Sad?"

"Yes, you see . . ." And at this his voice trailed off to a very soft choking, crying noise. Benjie waited, not knowing what to do, for this was very strange.

"You see," the voice continued, "my *inside* isn't as sure as my *outside* is. Everything I have going for me is all on the surface, you might say."

"But, Mr. Black Sheep," Benjie protested, "if you change the outside, or if your outside is what you want, won't the inside follow right along?"

"For me it hasn't happened. Maybe for you it would."

At this there followed several minutes of silence. Over on the right of them a three-year-old named Shuman was snoring quite loudly. No one knew where he picked up this detestable habit, but most believe it was Cragmire who had given Shuman the idea.

On the left the prettiest of the ewes, with the exception of Lana Lee, were huddled together. For their own protection, they said. Yet Gridley was the only ram who ever paid them any attention.

Lana Lee was considered a snob by the other pretty ewes because she didn't hang out with them. Actually, she was very shy and didn't care to gossip all day long about that ram, or this ewe, and on and on.

On the crest of the hill Mr. and Mrs. Alexander Ram slept comfortably, and over them—very far away—myriads of twinkling stars threw a cover over the entire flock.

Benjamin raised his head and counted the stars in his favorite constellation. There were always the same number, but just in case one fell he had to check every now and then.

Sometimes he wondered if there were stars so far away he simply couldn't see them, but there were so many now this thought seemed a little silly. And besides, even if there were only a dozen stars in the sky, the idea of something being there that couldn't be seen was, by itself, utterly ridiculous.

As sleep began to demand his attention, Benjamin turned once more to his neighbor.

"Mr. Black Sheep?"

"Yes?"

"I know you won't laugh if I tell you this, but . . . but I'm going to change my fleece into a pure white."

The black sheep wasted no time in replying, but even raised his voice a little louder than those sleeping would have liked.

"If you'll stand next to me in the day," he said, "it *will* look pure white."

"Hey, I never thought of . . ."

"But, Benjamin," he quickly went on, "if you stand next to the brightest white you'll still look very, very gray. It all depends which way you view things."

"Oh."

Suddenly Benjie's dream of turning his coat into something which would be worshiped by Gridley and all the others became a very confused tangle of desire and fear.

After all, the black sheep had achieved his own kind of perfection in his fleece, but became all bothered by the inside and the outside and all that stuff.

If Benjamin obtained *his* dream, would he be bothered?

It must have been early morning. Long before Cragmire would build his fire to ward off the chill or the baby lambs would nestle up to their mothers for a soothing drink of warm milk.

Benjie's eyes were weighed down with sleep, yet his mind was very alert.

Then, ever so softly, a voice spoke.

"Benjamin Alexander Sheep!"

"What do you want, Mr. Black Sheep?" Benjie sleepily replied.

"I'm not Mr. Black Sheep."

Benjamin tried to shake the wool from his eyes and stare into the blackness, but all he saw were the resting forms of the others as their bodies rose slightly up and down with each breath.

Seeing no one else who was awake, Benjie dropped his head.

"Benjamin."

"Huh?" This time he was quite awake. "Is that you, Cragmire?"

"No."

"Pardon me. I thought it was the shepherd."

"It is."

Perhaps he wasn't awake after all, Benjie

thought. Otherwise he wouldn't be hearing a voice which came from an invisible sheep or man. Besides, there had never been, in his life time, another shepherd other than Cragmire.

"If . . . if you're there," Benjie asked, "why can't I see you?"

"Do you hear my voice?"

"Yes."

"Then, for now, that is proof enough of my existence."

Benjie not only heard the voice, but he almost became overpowered by it. Not because of its volume, for it was very delicate, but because of its strange quality of tenderness and bold authority. Kind, but firm.

"What do you want?"

"With all respect, Benjamin," the voice said, "what do *you* want?" Benjie had a feeling the voice already knew, but he answered him anyway.

"I want a . . . pure white fleece, Mr. . . . Mr. . . .?"

"My name is Chaiyim."

"Chaiyim? What does that mean?"

"If you're truly curious enough, you'll find out. Yet there are more important things to discuss. Why do you want a white fleece?"

"So that stupid Gridley and the others will respect me. Even worship me, maybe."

At this the voice remained very silent, allowing Benjie's last statement to become heavier and heavier on his conscience until the weight was almost unbearable. He didn't know why, but after talking with this voice he knew he had been wanting his new fleece for the wrong reason.

"Er, Mr. Chaiyim, are you still there?"

"Yes."

"You think I've been heading for the wrong pasture, so to speak, don't you?"

46

"I think you've already answered that."

"Oh."

A deliciously cool breeze swept across his face, bringing an unusual refreshment to the conversation. It was at this point Benjamin realized the other sheep were not disturbed by the talking. But why?

The answer caused him to tremble. Benjamin Alexander Sheep had been casually speaking without opening his mouth or uttering a sound! It seemed as if they were speaking normally, yet in fact their thoughts sped back and forth with no help from vocal cords.

"Benjamin," the voice continued, "have you had any luck in turning your fleece to a pure white?"

"Certainly you must know."

"Just answer the question."

"No. Course not. But I haven't tried *everything* yet."

"Ah, I see. What else do you propose to do?"

"Well, I could . . . could *think* my way into a new fleece! They say sheep are very dumb, you know, so there must be a lot of room for improvement. Concentration, that's it! I've simply got to concentrate!"

"Fine, Benjamin. What will you concentrate on?"

"Why, myself of course!"

Once more there was no immediate reply. Benjie's thoughts drifted from one thing to another. Is he really dreaming? Is it some trick Cragmire is playing on me? No, Cragmire could never produce a voice like that—and without speaking out loud.

He gazed up the slope toward his sleeping father, the mighty ram. He was one of the wisest in the flock, but would he know the answer to this? Perhaps he should wake him.

As Benjamin stretched his back legs and

yawned he had to discard this idea. Waking his father in the middle of the night and asking him what he thought of a conversation he was having with someone who couldn't be seen wasn't a smart thing to do.

By not answering, did the voice agree with him? That if he concentrated on himself he could accomplish his goal? There was only one way to find out.

Benjamin turned all of his attention inward. He thought of how he outmaneuvered his twin sister for the best spot at his mother's belly during feeding time.

He remembered Cragmire picking him up when he was only a few weeks old and crudely spreading his fingers apart as he felt the wool— not keeping them together for a more gentle touch.

Benjie visualized Lana Lee and how beautiful she was. A little flaky, maybe, but pretty. He

couldn't recall a day when he hadn't known her.

Oooooops, wrong track, Benjie, he thought. You're supposed to be thinking about *you,* not Lana Lee. Concentrate on *yourself* and *your* beauty, not hers.

OK. On Benjie. What a fine ram he would be! Larger than his father, maybe, with horns everyone would admire. A natural leader of the flock. Except for Cragmire.

Cragmire! He certainly would never win any shepherd-of-the-year award. What a genuine meanie! Yech. Benjie hated him and everything he did. What a rotten shepherd he was. Benjie wished he would be replaced by another.

Hey! Wait a minute! There was another, wasn't there? Sure, the voice! The voice had said he was a shepherd. Yet if this was true, then where was his flock? Where were his lambs, ewes and rams?

Aw, that wouldn't work. What good would

it do to have a shepherd you couldn't even see?

Benjie sighed a great sigh and relaxed his muscles. Why wasn't he sleepy? This was very unusual. He'd probably be wiped out the next day and would have to take a nap just as the newborn ones did.

The night had almost passed. As the eastern sun very gradually began to paint streaks across the distant horizon it dawned on Benjie that he hadn't been able to accomplish anything by concentrating on himself.

Even his concentrating had been wishy-washy in its attentiveness to its prime subject—himself. Then, hope against hope, the sweet, fluid voice spoke once more.

"Benjamin. The light is gradually creeping skyward."

"Chaiyim!"

"How did your concentrating go?"

"Not very well."

"Then what will you do next?"

Benjie had not thought about this. The worst thing in the world to happen to him would be to have his options closed. With no alternative plan he would have to abandon his dream. Yet he would rather die than do that. There had to be a way.

"I . . . I don't know. Do you?"

"Perhaps."

"Maybe I can't think of it because I'm only a sheep."

"Only a sheep?" Chaiyim said. "I think more of you than that. Not even earth's shepherds have all the answers."

"Not shepherds like Cragmire, anyway."

"No, not like him. Cragmire is simply one of many. A shepherd."

"Same as you, I suppose?"

"Not quite, Benjamin. I said I was *the* shepherd."

"Oh."

Benjamin said "oh" as if he understood, because he didn't want to sound stupid. Nothing really made much sense to him, but he didn't want the voice to think he was dumb. This would only serve to support the reputation his fellow sheep already had.

"There's a rumor," Benjamin said, "that several years ago Cragmire lost almost a third of his entire flock overnight. They only let him go because the same thing happened to other shepherds at the same time, although some lost more than others.

"Cragmire's boss thought he had sold his best lambs on the side to smugglers, but they discovered many of the puniest sheep were also missing, so they were puzzled."

"Yes, I know," the voice said.

"You mean it's true?" Benjamin asked.

"Benjamin. Are you really interested in finding the truth?"

Here we go again, Benjie thought. More questions. Questions which seemed to lead him to new understandings which didn't particularly feel comfortable. Yet if this stranger knew something which Benjie didn't, he might as well listen. Who knows? Maybe he'd learn the secret to having a white fleece.

"Yeah, sure, Chaiyim. I'd really like to learn the truth."

"You don't sound very enthusiastic."

"That's because . . . may I be honest?"

"Of course."

"It's because when a sheep learns something new there's usually something to do in return. You know, strings attached and all that."

"No strings. Honest."

"OK," Benjie said, "then how can I find truth?"

"By trusting me. Getting to know me. Look to the east, Benjamin. With each moment the light becomes brighter."

"This is all so crazy," Benjamin complained. "I admit I'm troubled and anxious and confused all at once. Yet how—how can I trust a shepherd I haven't seen? How can . . ."

"You've heard my voice, Benjamin. When I hear yours I'll return."

As the sheep groggily stumbled to their feet the dazzling rays of the day-star threw deep black shadows to the front of them. One by one, yet almost together, the members of the flock rose and began searching for a decent breakfast.

The yearling lay very still, its eyelids tightly shut and a million sounds and pictures racing through its mind. Cragmire, approaching quietly over the grass with a lifted crook, slammed down his wooden shaft with a mighty blow on the yearling's rump.

And Benjamin Alexander Sheep, not knowing if this was the end of a horrible nightmare or the beginning of a cherished dream, scrambled wildly from his hill in pursuit of fresh grass, clear water and truth.

Part Three

Benjie was irritable.
Really irritable. Cragmire had been pushing him around most of the day and Lana Lee said she couldn't talk to him when he was so "moody."

Maybe it was due to the fact he hadn't slept much, or because he felt so alienated from the rest of the flock. Benjamin's unrest could have been caused by any number of things, but in any case he had to find a release for his imprisoned emotions.

Cragmire became the perfect target.

The past few months Benjie had seen a few adult rams knock their heads together over food or a ewe or something like that. They would lower their heads, build up speed and KA-POWIE! It was really something to watch.

Just as he was daydreaming about these

forceful acts of power he noticed Cragmire kneeling by the rapidly moving stream, the shepherd's head hovering close over the water as he cupped his hands for a drink.

The temptation became too great. Cragmire, with his back turned toward Benjie, had humbled himself to a position of great vulnerability. The large area covered in part by his back pockets seemed to call out for Benjie to act.

Benjie quickly glanced to his right and left, but the others were so busy eating they wouldn't notice. He grinned to himself and positioned his head at just the right level. His feet dug into the soft turf and Benjie sped down a bumpy slope.

He was right on course. The swiftness with which he ran was aided by an overpowering urge for revenge and satisfaction. At the last second Cragmire, hearing him come, looked over his shoulder.

It was too late. THWACK! OOOOOF! SPLASH!

The lanky shepherd went somersaulting headfirst into the river, his feet thrashing in the air before disappearing for a moment beneath the surface. He quickly surfaced, spewing water from his mouth, and stared with disbelief at Benjie.

Who, unlike his plan to immediately flee, was in convulsive fits of laughter.

"Hah! Wooo-eee! Cragmire, you look so stupid! Ah, hah!" Benjamin laughed and laughed as Cragmire climbed onto the land and very deliberately picked up a crook which had been resting on the bank of the stream.

At the sight of the crook Benjie's laughter faded to a sudden stop. The reality of that huge shepherd and his staff almost upon him shocked Benjie into action and he turned to run away.

Swish! Before he could make good his escape

Cragmire had whipped his crook through Benjie's back feet and sent him sprawling tail-over-nose across the pasture. Before the lamb could regain his feet Cragmire was over him, sending blow after blow upon his body before dragging him across the rockiest part of the field to the main camp.

The corral was scarcely big enough for a lamb to lie down in. It was composed of a crude wood fence made of three horizontal beams around the four sides.

This was the punishment cell. The first time Benjie had ever been placed there. Hour after hour, with no water and the naked dirt ground offering him no food, Benjie gazed with vacant eyes toward the distant hills.

Why did pleasure which lasted for so short a time result in punishment which went on and

on with seemingly no end in sight? Yet punishment which lasted but a brief moment in time
wouldn't be punishment at all, Benjie thought.
Cragmire, though, had to be unusually cruel.

No food or water. No visitors. And constant
watching.

Once, when Benjie heard a familiar grumbling
from his stomach, he attempted to squeeze his
head under the bottom rail and nip some grass
which was growing just past the outside perim-
eter.

At the point where his head was almost stuck
because of the narrowness of the opening, but
before he could reach the grass, Cragmire's staff
fell heavily on Benjie's nose.

"Baaaa!" Benjie cried.

"That'll teach you," Cragmire said.

By evening Cragmire had lifted his restriction
on visitors. After having spoken with no one

the entire day and hungry for conversation, the yearling was stunned to hear the first one to address him.

"Hey, runt! What's mommy's little lamb done now?"

It was Gridley. A cocky smile split his wide face and he pressed close to the corral, his eyes staring proudly through the space between the second and third beams.

"Go away, Gridley."

"Nah, I think it'd be more fun if *you'd* try to go away!"

At this Gridley stretched out, snipped a clump of fine grass with his teeth and made as many slurpy noises as he could.

"You shouldn't make Cragmire mad like that, sonny," Gridley said, "or he'll be on your back the rest of your life. What a shame, huh?" Gridley shoved a few blades of grass just under the fence and put his hoof on top of it. "Try and

get," he said. Benjamin looked from the grass to Gridley's horns.

"Go away, Gridley."

"Look at that, will you," Gridley sneered, "the baby ram is telling me to go away! First he insults the only shepherd we've got and then he tells a *superior* to go away! I'll say one thing, Benjie baby, you've got a lot of guts."

"How do you know," Benjie said in a rather distant way, "that Cragmire is the only shepherd we've got?"

Gridley looked puzzled at Benjie, raised his head toward the sky and squinted.

"Sun was hot today, is that it? The sun's got to you?"

"Yeah, maybe it's the sun."

But it wasn't the heat or anything else, Benjie thought. And it happened at night when the land was cool and free from distractions. When a sheep's mind could grasp smells, sounds and even thoughts which always seemed to be crowded out of a busy day's awareness.

"My dear Benjamin," Gridley continued with a phony formality, "I have never known, nor ever heard of, another shepherd other than Cragmire. And if you think *you* have then I . . ." Gridley laughed quite rudely. "I *demand* you show him to me!"

"Even if he were to show himself," Benjie said with a faint touch of sympathy, "I don't think you'd see him. At least—not the way I do."

"Do? You do see him? Reminds me of a stage I went through. Poor, poor Benjie. Cragmire's crook must really have taken its toll."

Gridley stood, and, shaking his head in wonder, trotted away.

As the night became crisp and sweet Benjamin

tossed restlessly in the corral. He pictured himself by the river, bloated with water and feasting on a long, tasty carrot. Or in an undiscovered valley where the grass seemed to drip with salt and white, fleecy clouds would spell out "BENJAMIN" in the sky.

Then again he may be standing with Lana Lee and dozens of other pretty ewes, with the finest curved horns in the history of rams growing proudly from his head and shining in the palest moonlight.

Or perhaps he would . . .

"Benjamin?" Benjie picked up his ears. "Benjie?"

"Lana Lee! Why didn't you come earlier?"

"Shhhh! Not so loud!"

"Aw, for the . . ."

"Please! I'm afraid."

"Of what?"

"Shhhh!"

Lana Lee's body tensed and her ears twitched with concentration. After a few impatient moments she turned back to Benjie.

"You can't be too careful, you know. If Cragmire knew I was here he'd throw me in there too."

"That may not be a bad idea," Benjie chuckled.

"Benjamin!"

"Shhhh!" he mocked her.

Lana Lee pressed close to the wooden barrier and listened while Benjie's eyes hopped from one shadow to the next. Neither noticed anything unusual.

"I heard you butted Cragmire," Lana whispered, "that was a foolish thing to do. Gridley's been telling everyone you've seen another shepherd and I just don't understand why you insist on saying these things and . . ."

"Lana! Hush up for once, will you?"

"But, Benjie, you can't actually *see* the other shepherd and I think it's time you knew that."

It was more the urgency in her voice than what she actually had said which added a spark to this silly ewe's gibberish. Just as before, it seemed Lana Lee was trying to circle around something, or someone she knew but was afraid to pinpoint.

"What shepherd?" he said cautiously.

"Why, the one you told Gridley you saw!"

"I never told him I had *seen* the shepherd, Lana Lee."

"Oh! Well, I've got to go. If I don't get more sleep tonight my wool will look a *mess* tomorrow! G'night!"

"LANA! Wait!"

He strained his eyes for a last glimpse of her, but could not raise his voice any louder for fear Cragmire would hear him. Drat that goofy lamb, he thought. Then, from behind him, Benjie heard more hoofsteps.

"Lana?" he breathed.

"No," a husky voice replied, "not quite." Benjie twisted around.

"Father!"

The majestic ram stood courageously by a section of shaky wooden beams which, when loosed, provided the entrance—and exit—to the corral. Benjie felt an immediate rush of security from seeing his father's stately figure and bobbing horns.

And with a sense of imminent freedom there came a deluge of apprehension. If he did escape, what then? What would Cragmire do? Not only to him, but to his father?

Mr. Alexander Ram gracefully knocked his

horns against the top beam to test its strength.

"Father, wait!"

"What is it, son?" He pointed his left horn toward Benjie.

"Maybe this isn't such a good idea."

"Don't you want to be free?"

"Yes, but . . ."

THUD. The top beam hit the dirt right at Benjie's feet. THUD. Working quickly, the ram had swiftly butted his head against the middle beam and sent it crashing upon the first.

"Jump, son!"

The ram bolted off into the darkest of the shadows as a confused Benjie heard a *clinking* sound behind him. He saw a swish of light, like a flattened out "U," steadily approaching him. Cragmire's lantern!

There was no time for thought. Benjie easily leaped over the bottom beam and ran in the

same direction his father had gone. As he flew across the meadow Cragmire's raspy voice struck out like a lightning bolt.

"I'll get you for this! I'll get you good!"

Benjie had never run so far or so fast in his life. His eyes had already adjusted themselves to the faint light of the evening and he only stumbled once or twice.

The fire he felt in his lungs now burned with a new intensity as his breaths came short and hard. An uncomfortable thumping pounded in his chest and his legs ached.

He finally allowed himself the luxury of glancing back. There was no light, no sound, no trace of Cragmire. Benjamin, terrible hunger and thirst demanding his attention, fell to the ground on top of a damp knoll, unable to move.

Perhaps thirty minutes had passed. Maybe an hour. Benjamin lay still on the knoll, his mind unable to release his body into a desperately needed sleep.

He thought of how brave his father had been. Of fresh flowers and crystal clear water. He pictured Cragmire beating him to a woolly pulp. A reddish, pinkish sunset which seemed to resist the beckoning night streaked across his memory, then faded to a twinkling blackness.

Benjie was counting the stars in his constellation. All there. At least that hadn't changed.

If only the night would last forever. If only the light of morning wouldn't expose him to the shepherd's vengeful eye and bring him more grief than he could bear.

The soreness of his muscles, emptiness of his stomach and parched tongue somehow stimulated Benjie's thought processes. As if weakness in his flesh gave life to his soul and intellect.

He shivered. The cold of darkness increased and Benjie began to yearn for a skin to be thrown

over him. Fat chance of that happening, though. With the shepherd his number one enemy.

Wait now, he mused. *Cragmire wasn't the* only *shepherd, was he? What about Chaiyim?* Ah, phooey. An invisible shepherd would probably have invisible skins with him.

Each minute brought him closer and closer to a showdown with Cragmire, and he would be no good in battle if he was half frozen. Benjie felt helpless, his reliance on himself at an embarrassing low.

Ah, Chaiyim, he thought, *if only you could do something. If you're real, then please help. Somebody. Somebody's got to help me.*

The cold which had been nipping at his legs began to leave him, and his body slowly rocked to a peaceful stillness from its frantic shivering. A very special warmth, as if he was snuggled between two fat ewes on a winter's night, touched every part of Benjie's body.

"Hello, Benjamin Alexander. Nice to hear from you."

"Huh?"

At first Benjie panicked, thinking it was Cragmire, but when he came to his senses he realized what was happening.

"Chaiyim!"

"At your service."

"But I've said nothing out loud! I didn't call you!"

"I listen to the heart, Benjamin, not the tongue."

"Oh."

It was the same kind of "oh" Benjie had used before with Chaiyim, for he understood—but not much. The invisible shepherd had promised to return when he heard Benjie's voice, yet it had only taken a few words spoken in silence from the heart to do this.

"Now, my young friend," Chaiyim said, "what can I do for you?"

"To tell you the truth, sir, I really don't know."

"Didn't you want a white, white fleece?"

"Yeah, sure, but that's changed a little maybe. As far as priorities go."

"How do you mean?"

"Chaiyim, a bright white fleece will do me no good if the shepherd kills me right after I get it."

"I've told you before, Benjamin, I am the shepherd."

There he goes again. Why all this double talk? He liked to play games as much as Lana Lee. But there was a big difference. Lana Lee was afraid to tell him the answer while Chaiyim was anxious to say more but always seemed to insist on Benjie probing him with a sincere kind of persistence.

"How do you mean, sir?" Benjie asked.

"Just because a man is a shepherd and has a flock doesn't mean he speaks the whole truth. Half-truths, maybe, or lies."

"All I know," Benjie sighed, "is that I can't take being a prisoner any longer. I'll never go back to that pen."

"But, Benjamin," Chaiyim said with great patience, "you're a prisoner *now*."

Benjie, startled, lifted his front feet and surveyed the land which circled his knoll. He only felt the freshest of winds, saw a countryside completely at rest and smelled the smells of moist earth and trampled grass.

"I see no one, Chaiyim," Benjie said, "am I your prisoner?"

"No."

"Then whose prisoner am I?"

"You're a prisoner, Benjamin, of yourself."

At this the warmth which had taken the chill

from his body seeped deeper and deeper within him until he felt tiny beads of sweat form on his skin. It was a very different kind of heat from that which the sun poured out.

"I—I don't understand," Benjie whimpered.

"Dear, dear Benjamin," Chaiyim said, "if only you would stop running long enough to really look at yourself. You're your own prisoner because your dreams far exceed your ability to achieve them.

"No matter how many different ways you try to change the color of your fleece it simply can't be done. No matter how hard you put your mind to it, you would never lose the hatred you feel for Gridley and Cragmire."

"But, Chaiyim!" Benjie protested, "Gridley is such a bad ram! And Cragmire is a rotten shepherd! You almost said so yourself! Certainly I have a right to hate them!"

"Tell me, Benjamin. Would you like to see

a perfect world? Where the shepherds loved their flocks without expecting anything in return, and the sheep loved their shepherds because they loved them first?"

"Yes."

"And would you like to see a world where there were plenty of turnips for all and cool, clear water springing up everywhere and each sheep would be at peace with himself and with others?"

"Why, yes, of course, but . . ."

"Benjamin Alexander Sheep. May I ask yet another question? May I ask if at least you, on your own, have attained the kind of selfless perfection needed to make this kind of world work?"

"Of course not, Chaiyim, but it's perfection I'd like to strive for."

"Then if you're not perfect," Chaiyim said, "you've lost your right to hate."

It was no longer possible for Benjie to determine where Chaiyim's voice was coming from. It had long ceased to be something with volume, something spoken out loud. He felt a transparent cloud of sound surrounding him, as if to comfort as well as instruct.

Benjie's mind skipped about a whole slate of ideas and emotions. As soon as he had landed on one thought he'd be jumping off to another, then back again. No right to hate? Unable to achieve perfection? Cragmire a (how would you say it?) *false* shepherd?

Then if Cragmire, and others Benjie didn't know, were false shepherds, and Chaiyim was *the* shepherd, then Chaiyim must be the *true* shepherd.

Unless, of course, Chaiyim was a liar and Cragmire was actually a pretty good guy. No, that seemed all wrong. A certain quality in Chaiyim's voice demonstrated an unusual discipline with love, much like his father had spoken to him, but with a depth his father didn't have.

Perhaps a few more questions would straighten things out.

"Chaiyim?"

"Yes, Benjamin?"

"Is there any way, is it *possible,* for me to ever earn a pure white fleece?"

"To earn it, no. To receive it, yes."

"How?"

"By being set free."

"But you said I was a prisoner of myself. How could I ever become free of me?"

"By believing, Benjamin. By believing in me, and what I've done. Only I can release you."

"But you can't mean . . ."

"By joining my flock, Benjamin," Chaiyim said, "you'll receive complete freedom."

"And what about my white fleece?"

"Yes, and a pure white fleece!" Chaiyim laughed.

"I'm still a little mixed up, sir," Benjamin said, "but I can't fight this feeling I have. I believe as much as you've told me. I want your kind of freedom."

"Then surely as my name is Chaiyim," he said, "you're mine."

These last words lingered in Benjie's heart as he closed his eyelids and shifted to a more comfortable position on the knoll. He thought of the black sheep and for the first time understood all of that inside-outside stuff.

For Benjie was positive his inside was now very, very white and someday soon his fleece would be too.

Part Four

Benjie circled around
the outside of the flock, wedging himself between two larger sheep and melting into the
others as much as possible. Cragmire was
scolding one of his sheep dogs on the other
side of the crowd.

"Hey, Benjamin! I thought you were . . ."

"Shhh! Keep your voice down, dummy."

It was Shuman, the three-year-old who snored
at night and made a nuisance of himself in the
daytime. No one ever paid much attention to
Shuman, or spent the time to discover what his
thoughts were. If, in fact, he thought at all.

"If he finds you it's going to be all over,"
Shuman said.

"That's a pretty big *if*, Shuman."

"Not really." Shuman's tongue licked a few

blades of grass which clung to his foot. "Sooner or later the shepherd always finds who he's looking for."

"I can believe that about the shepherd," Benjie said, "but not Cragmire."

"So who do you think Cragmire is? A grasshopper?"

What's the use, Benjie thought. Shuman would never understand. Or would he? Yet it seemed only fair he should have the chance to meet Chaiyim just as Benjie had.

"A funny thing happened to me last night," Benjie began.

"Yeah, the whole flock knows. Your father sprung you from the pen."

"I mean after that."

"Let me guess. You fell into a ripe pile of mangels?"

"No."

"A rotten pile?"

"What's the use, Shuman. You'd never understand."

"Understand what, Benjamin? That you've
been knocked in the head one time too many?"

"No," Benjie said quietly, "that there's another
shepherd other than Cragmire. And he can make
you pure white inside."

"There," Shuman laughed, "you've just proved
my point." He studied Benjie's head. "The lumps
must have gone down, though!"

Benjie checked out Cragmire's position. Still
safe. The dogs had gone about their business
of rounding up strays and everything seemed
peaceful. By this time Shuman had moved away
and was speaking in a hush-hush voice to another ram while nodding at Benjie. Let him have
his fun, Benjie decided, someday Chaiyim would
teach him a thing or two.

The young ram's thoughts wandered for too
long a time, for Cragmire had circled the flock

and was rapidly approaching Benjie's position.

"You troublesome little runt," Cragmire yelled, "now you'll be sorry!"

At the sound of his biting voice the other sheep moved clumsily away from Benjamin.

"He's his own sheep!" one cried.

"I'd never listen to him!" a ewe bleated.

"You're on your own, Benjie!" another yelled.

Yet Cragmire could not understand sheep talk that well, so for him it came out:

"Baaaaa!"

"Baaa! Baaa!"

"Baaaaaaaa!"

Which, of course, meant nothing to him. But something Benjie did must have surprised him a great deal, as it did the entire flock. For instead of trying to run away, or cower behind the others, Benjamin Alexander Sheep stood his ground and faced the tall, stringy shepherd.

"You're a horrible shepherd!" Benjie said with a loud, quivering voice. "You have no right trying to lead us! And you can easily be replaced by an invisible shepherd whom I've met!"

For Cragmire the spunky little lamb had merely cut loose with a whole series of bleats, but the flock listened to the most remarkable speech ever passed down from ewe to lamb.

"I've always wanted a pure white fleece, Cragmire," Benjie continued, "but it became obvious that I couldn't earn it by myself. Besides, a fleece like that must begin in the inside and finally end up on the outside. If you knew Chaiyim you'd know what I was talking about!"

Benjie knew that only his own kind could understand him. It was his desperate hope that some would want to know more. And if they did he certainly couldn't speak if Cragmire got hold of him, slapped him in the pen and forbid visitors from coming.

"Enough of that noise! Your time has come!"

An overflowing rush of urgency swelled within Benjie's heart and he decided it would be better to die than to become a prisoner of the wrong shepherd. Cragmire had his staff, but Benjie had the element of surprise working for him.

"Baaaaa!" Benjie screamed at Cragmire, then raced headfirst straight at the shepherd. Cragmire, shocked, raised his crook high over his head.

"You can't stop me, Cragmire!" Benjie said, then abruptly planted his four hoofs into the ground and skidded to a sudden stop about five feet in front of the angry man. Cragmire, his timing thrown off, cracked his staff in two as it smashed against the ground.

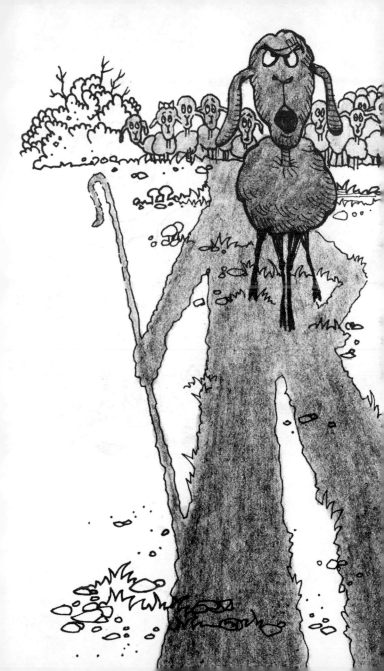

Just as quickly Benjie darted toward Cragmire, leaped between his knees and sent him toppling in the dirt. The lamb, to the amazement of all, sprinted to freedom over a nearby rise.

That night Benjie listened for two sounds. One he feared, the other he yearned for. The first was the expected footsteps of Cragmire and the clink of his lantern. The second was the sweet voice of Chaiyim.

Neither came.

The next morning his wool was heavily coated with dew. After a quick drink at the river and a hasty breakfast of coarse grass and weed, Benjie set off on a task he felt inwardly compelled to complete.

He must, in any way possible, tell the others about Chaiyim. He wasn't sure how he might accomplish this, but knew he must try. Many would react as Shuman had, with complete disbelief. Their entire existence consisted of eating, drinking and Cragmire.

For others, those who wanted to look forward to something more eventful than having their wool sheared off, there was a whole new world waiting. Now and forever.

Ah, Chaiyim, Benjie thought, *please show me the way.* The young one was still, disappointed he had heard no reply, and when the answer came about an hour later he didn't recognize it as such.

Benjie had felt as if he was playing one of the baby lambs' games, hide-a-sheep, when a stray nearly collided with him. It had been following its nose, never looking where it was going, and offered a sharp contrast to the pastel colors of the meadow.

"Why, hello, Mr. Black Sheep!" Benjie said.

"Huh? Oh!" The sheep bolted.

"Stop! Mr. Black Sheep, please stop!"

Benjie's voice, full of compassion, captured the fleeing sheep and he tip-toed to within a short distance of his friend.

"This is highly unusual for me," Black Sheep said.

"Likewise, I'm sure," answered Benjie. "But I won't make fun of you. Promise."

"Then . . . then what do you want?"

It was a lovely hour. Benjie began by relating his own experiences with Chaiyim, to which Black Sheep had only replied Benjamin was either the greatest storyteller in the world or it was, indeed, the truth.

There followed much discussion about fleeces, shepherds, peace and joy. Benjie didn't actually hear Chaiyim's voice, but so many beautiful thoughts and deep insights flowed from his lips that he couldn't take credit himself.

He knew, in his own right, he wasn't that wise.

Black Sheep was the first. Then came the others. At first they came one by one, then by twos and threes. Benjie stood on the top of a small knoll and answered as many questions as he could.

He didn't know all of the answers, but was sure this was due to his not knowing Chaiyim as well as he should, rather than there being no answer at all.

The thing which astounded Benjie the most was that in spite of all the similarities the sheep had, they also had great differences. And by the answers which seemed involuntarily to form in his mind, it seemed Chaiyim was intent on enriching the positive traits of the sheep, each in its own way, rather than mold them all into a common personality as Cragmire had tried to do.

Yet with every sheep who came to believe in Chaiyim as the true shepherd there were many who did not.

"You're as looney as a ladybug with sunstroke," one called out.

"You're too young to know what you're talking about!"

"Children's made-up stories!"

"Absurd!"

"Ridiculous!"

Those who had come to believe remained quiet, listening to Benjie gently instruct them in the magic of faith and trust in Chaiyim.

"I can't say exactly how it works," Benjie said, "but it does. All you have to do is try it and you'll know. But you have to trust."

There were about one hundred sheep jammed around the tiny orator, and although Benjie knew this might arouse the suspicion of Cragmire he kept right on speaking. And speaking.

And speaking. Until the rebels in the crowd bleated with such an ear-shattering racket that it brought Cragmire on the run to find out what was happening.

"So!"

"Cragmire!"

"The party's over, runt. For good!"

"Throw him to the dogs!" one of the disbelievers said.

"Yes, throw him to the dogs. He'd make four fine legs of lamb for you, Cragmire!"

"Legs of lamb!" another echoed.

A few faithful followers attempted to push Benjie through the crowd and protect him but the others would have no part of this. They squeezed as tightly as they could into a giant sheep-jam and refused to let Benjie escape. Only Cragmire was allowed to pass in their midst. Benjie couldn't move.

Cragmire's new staff, much thicker than his

old one, rained blow after blow upon Benjie, from his bleeding nose to his broken back left leg. Tufts of wool were ripped off by the pounding and soon the yearling's eyes were swollen far beyond the black rims of hair which circled them. Benjie, his head spinning and throbbing all at once, peered dizzily through fleshy slits.

Cragmire pulled a rope from his back pocket and wrapped it tightly around Benjie's middle, just behind his front legs. The shepherd knew he could take full advantage of the lamb by dragging him over the stony ground.

The last thing Benjie remembered before he fell unconscious, remembered even more than the acute pain from his leg, was the nasty, jeering sheep which continued to mock him even as he slipped ever so close to death.

Thick staffs. Ugly sheep. Tear-filled eyes of believers. Grass. Knoll. Sky. Rope. Ummmmph.

Benjie felt a cool, refreshing whisp of air swoop low into the pen. It was impossible to tell how many hours had passed, but by straining to see through his puffy eyes Benjie could tell it was very dark.

With a tremendous effort he lifted his head for a glimpse of his favorite constellation. His eyes must be playing tricks on him, he thought. Once more, the pain ripping at his muscles, Benjie forced his head higher.

It wasn't there! His constellation was gone! And—and so were the others! Check again. Eyes open? Yes, eyes open. Looking up? Yes, looking up. Constellations and stars there? Nope. Not there. Then what . . . ?

"I see you still have life left in you!" a voice barked. "We'll take care of that!"

It was Cragmire, followed by several of the more hostile sheep. He was carrying a handful of something which he threw into the pen so it landed right in front of Benjie's nose.

"Here. A last noon meal for the condemned!"

It was a squished mound of weeds, turnips and fat beets. All dry or rotten and crawling with several types of slinky bugs. Benjie turned his head as much as he could and, when he did, saw something he hadn't noticed before.

Dogs. Two ferocious dogs tied to a corner post and standing, waiting, just outside the pen. So he, in turn, was to provide a meal for others.

If only this hadn't happened. If he had only minded his own business and gone along with the flock he would have been just fine. Ow! His leg. It was really acting up now and sent bolts of pain shooting through his whole body.

And what of Chaiyim? Why did the shepherd leave him to the mercy of Cragmire? Is that what you call caring for your lambs?

The thought of being deserted by a trusted friend hurt Benjie a great deal more than did the thought of imminent death by the jaws of two wild dogs. He winced. A noon meal, indeed. Why doesn't he get it over with?

The sheep standing with Cragmire had the same kind of look in their eyes. Awful. Just awful. There was one, standing in the very back, who had bowed its head as though a trifle ashamed of the proceedings. It was Shuman! And at the very moment Benjie recognized him something Cragmire had said captured his imagination.

"Shuman!" The ram started to turn. "Wait! I have to ask you something!" Shuman, having been noticed, decided to cooperate.

"Yeah?"

"Cragmire called this slop my noon meal, but it's pitch black outside. What did he mean?"

"Just what he said. Your noon meal."

"In the middle of the night?"

"No, in the middle of the day. It happened as he pulled you across the field. All at once the sun kind of went *poof,* just like that. Cragmire said it was nothing to worry about."

"Has this ever happened before?"

"Not that I know of."

"Then what do you think happened? Has anyone . . ."

"Look!" Shuman murmured, "There. Up there!"

Just above the horizon, about where the moon should have been resting, a fiery, bright dot bounced in the sky as if it were a raft being carried by a calm sea. Benjie stretched his eyelids apart as much as possible.

"Is it the sun?" one ram asked.

"No, too bright."

"And too small," another said.

"Not for long, though."

The dot had by this time grown to the size

of a large star, then became as big as the moon—then surpassed the sun. Its brightness turned the darkened day into a sparkling land of glistening grass and no shadows.

"The glare! I can't stand the glare!" Cragmire sobbed. He had dropped his crook and was attempting to cover his eyes with his hands. It didn't bother Benjie at all.

The dogs howled wildly and several sheep ran off in fear of what seemed to be approaching doom. Benjie lay still, fascinated with what was happening. He didn't move. The ground beneath him heaved up and down and a giant rumbling rolled under the earth, cracking open the land and sending the beams of the pen flying from the corner posts.

The pen! It's down! Benjie scrambled over a fallen beam and leaped high in the air as the soft grass cushioned his feet. How sweet freedom was! How . . . his leg! His leg was all better!

And his eyes, and his bruises, and everything!

"Whoooopeee!" someone said.

"I don't believe it! Yes, I do! I do!"

"Look who's here!"

The light was brighter than the hottest sun, but yet comfortable. It seemed to radiate from a particular spot on the pasture which was not too far away. Benjie, excited about what had released him, ran to see. A tremendous gathering of sheep, in a wild celebration, surrounded the source of light.

"Benjamin! Oh, Benjamin!" It was Lana Lee, looking more magnificent and beautiful than ever. "He's come! He's really come! Everything will be all right now!"

"Who's come, Lana? Who?" Benjie stared directly at a shepherd, a most unusual kind of shepherd, who sat upon a great throne in the pasture. Thousands of sheep and other animals which had come with him had pure white

fleeces or coats. Each reflected, in varying de-
grees, the light which sprang from the throne.
Before Lana spoke Benjie knew.

"Chaiyim."

"You know him too, Lana! Why didn't you
ever say?" She dropped her head and shuffled
her front feet.

"I . . . I tried."

"Never mind It makes no difference now!
Chaiyim isn't just a shepherd and a deliverer, he's
a king!"

Many of the animals stood with Cragmire on
a far corner of the meadow. The anguish and
despair written upon their faces was so very,
very sad that Benjie could only look for a few
seconds.

Standing with Benjie was his father, mother,
the black sheep and—Benjie swallowed hard—
Gridley! "You mean Gridley knew Chaiyim? That
awful Gridley who . . ."

"Benjamin Alexander Sheep!" Benjie was startled. He faced the throne.

"Yes, sir? Chaiyim, sir?"

"My ways are not your ways. Even abused, ill-treated gifts remain gifts just the same.

"Those around me have been with me since the Great Swoosh or before. As you see, each has a pure white fleece or coat, although some are brighter than others.

"You, and the others who have not followed Cragmire, have begun a journey which will lead to the perfect fleece you have dreamed about. Now come. Taste the sweetness of the rutabagas I have brought for you."

And Benjamin Alexander Sheep, feeling all tingly inside as he drew near to the most loving shepherd in the universe, couldn't decide whether Chaiyim had actually winked or if he merely had something in his eye.

Epilogue

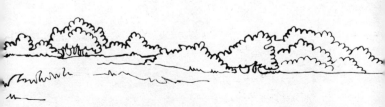

I first considered writing
Benjamin Alexander Sheep upon reading *Jonathan Livingston Seagull,* the best seller which, in my opinion, suggests to mankind everything it wants to believe about itself.

Jonathan Livingston Seagull appeared to be a weird mixture of Norman Vincent Peale, Napoleon Hill, Mary Baker Eddy and Gautama Siddhartha all packed into one neat little pill eagerly swallowed by those dreaming of being the captain of their own fate.

Richard Bach's philosophy, to my mind, is opposed, rather than complimentary, to what God says about the human race. It takes little imagination to see what he's getting at when he has Jonathan, his Christlike figure, saying:

"Don't let them spread silly rumors about me, or make me a god. O.K., Fletch? I'm a seagull. I like to fly, maybe . . ."

Bach could easily write a gospel account in which Jesus says:

125

"Don't let them spread silly rumors about me, or make me the Son of God. O.K., Peter? I'm an orator. I like to preach, maybe . . ."

On the last page of *Jonathan Livingston Seagull* the "truth" finally hits Fletcher, referred to as Jonathan's disciple, and he concludes "that his friend (Jonathan) had quite honestly been no more divine than Fletcher himself."

Ah! That's it! Once more we are told that God, or god, or whatever, is inside all of us—each a little god unto himself. By a rehashed version of positive thinking we can obtain *anything* by striving hard and really putting our mind to it.

If this were really true it appears there should have been some positive results long before now among greater numbers of persons. But for every man who "makes it" there are millions who struggle without hope from the maternity ward to the mausoleum.

And so I sent Benjamin out to pasture in an attempt to allow God to have equal time, or comment, according to what He has written in His Word.

When I was young I heard nothing about the Jewish concept of a Messiah during year after year of attending a reform temple. Then, through school and for a few years after, no Gentile ever told me Jesus had brought him love, hope and peace.

Just like Lana Lee. Lana Lee is, in truth, a believer who has so little real knowledge of her Lord that the slightest opposition thrown at her from the world frightens her from her faith. She knows, but is afraid to say

True believers in the Lord maintain we'll probably be surprised by at least two things once we're finally together in heaven: by who's there, and who isn't.

Mere man attempts to match himself with the holiness, righteousness and perfection of God and discovers he must fall short in the comparison. Both Old and New Testaments declare every man is a slave to sin, or rebellion, against God.

It became necessary for Jesus, a unique God-man truly free of sin, to redeem all others by

His personal sacrifice—to free humanity from its slavery. Who, being both God and man, is the only acceptable mediator between labor and management.

Yet most non-believers attempting to evaluate Christianity scrutinize professing "Christians" as true representatives of the faith.

I wanted to punch a few holes in this practice by using Gridley as my patsy. By believing in Jesus as the Messiah, and that He was, in fact, raised from the dead, a person can become a true child of God and receive, by grace, a spiritual clearance for eternity. Sadly, many ignore the promises and abundant life which Christ offers us *today*, and therefore follow Gridley as he becomes suffocated by secular values.

During the course of the book it is mentioned that at one time Cragmire, the false shepherd, had lost one-third of his flock in mysterious circumstances. Then, later, I refer to a Great Swoosh.

These items indicate what is termed the "rapture" by evangelical Christians. The rapture is an event in which the Bible states all those true believers in Christ, both dead and alive, will be transformed in a flash of an eyelid in order to meet the Lord together in the air.

For those remaining on earth it will mean the phone will go dead at the other end of the line, the driver of a car ahead of them in traffic will suddenly disappear or the man in charge of the missing person's desk will be missing.

Benjamin Alexander Sheep takes place *after* this event near the end of a seven-year period known as the tribulation. This will be a time of utter horror as man is given one last chance to believe Jesus is exactly who He says He is.

I represent the Lord, the true shepherd, as being *Chaiyim,* the Hebrew word for Life. Chaiyim is to be found in hundreds of messianic prophecies in the Old Testament, fulfilling them in the New Testament and is said to be coming to earth again as King—as indicated by both.

To me, Chaiyim, the everlasting Messiah Jesus, is the most wonderful hope and greatest joy modern man can experience. Chaiyim told Benjie:

"You've heard my voice, Benjamin. When I hear yours I'll return."

And, my friend, if *you* seek Chaiyim with all

your heart He'll not only hear, but He'll come,
and He'll answer.
So let us know, let us press on to know the LORD.
His going forth is as certain as the dawn;
And He will come to us like the rain,
Like the spring rain watering the earth.

(Hosea 6:3, *NASB*)